Becky Lennon

BARRY

THE FISH WITH FINGERS

Sue Hendra

Alfred A. Knopf

New York

THIS IS A BORZOI BOOK PUBLISHED BY ALFRED A. KNOPF

Copyright © 2010 by Sue Hendra

Knopf, Borzoi Books, and the colophon are registered trademarks of Random House, Inc.

Visit us on the Web! www.randomhouse.com/kids

Educators and librarians, for a variety of teaching tools, visit us at www.randomhouse.com/teachers

Library of Congress Cataloging-in-Publication Data
Hendra, Sue.
Barry, the fish with fingers / by Sue Hendra. — 1st ed.
p.   cm.
Summary: When Barry the fish shows off his new fingers, all the fish are eager to get their own.
ISBN 978-0-375-85894-9 (trade) — ISBN 978-0-375-95894-6 (lib. bdg.)
[1. Fishes—Fiction. 2. Fingers—Fiction.] I. Title.
PZ7.H3853Bar 2010
[E]—dc22
2009009888

The illustrations in this book were created using gouache.
Book concept by Paul Linnet and Sue Hendra.

MANUFACTURED IN CHINA
June 2010
10 9 8 7 6 5 4 3 2 1

First Edition

FOR MAX

Sea Slug liked to lie on the ocean floor and watch the fish swim by.

He did this every day.

He saw fat ones, thin ones, some as big as cars, some as small as buttons. Toothy ones, big-nosed ones, googly-eyed ones, spotty ones, stripy ones . . .

You name it, he'd seen it.

In fact, he thought he had seen it all . . .

. . . until he caught sight of Barry, that is.

"How do you do?" asked Barry, proudly waving his fish fingers.

"WOW! A fish with fingers!" exclaimed Sea Slug.

"These new fingers are the answer to every fish's problem," said Barry.

"What's *your* problem?" Barry asked
a moody-looking fish.

There was a long silence.

"I'm bored," said the fish.

"We're all bored," said the others.

"Well, prepared to be un-bored. . . ."

"Fingers mean

FINGER

"With fingers I can . . .

Knit a scarf!

Count to ten!

Type a letter!

Make a paper chain!

Finger-paint!

Play the piano!

Have a big morning stretch!"

"Fingers really are a must for tickling."

The fish could see why Barry loved his fingers.
They could do so *many* things!

Suddenly the sea went dark and
the water shook.

It was at that moment that one
of Barry's fingers did something
truly amazing. . . .

It pointed!

LOOK

Thanks to Barry's fast-acting finger, not a single fish got squished by the massive heavy box that fell into the sea.

Everyone cheered for Barry.

Hey, Barry, where can we get some of these fingers?

PIRATE JACK'S

TASTY
FISH STICKS

"Now I really *have* seen it all," said Sea Slug.